It was an angel's presence
that hovered by my bed.

Joy and sorrow filled my head.
I was alive. I wasn't dead.

Dead in life. Alive in death,
is not spoken of my breath.

~ Candice James
(Excerpt pg. 31)

Also, by Candice James

Print Books
A Split in the Water 2nd edition
Transitioning;
10 PAKs–5; 4; 3; 2; 1
A Potpourri of Paintings;
The Still Small Voice of Soul;
Spiritual Whispers; Atmospheres;
Blue Silence; Call of the Crow;
Imagination's Reverie; Short Shots 2;
The Depth of the Dance;
Behind the One-Way Mirror;
The Path of Loneliness
Rithimus Aeternam; The Water Poems;
Short Shots; City of Dreams;
Merging Dimensions; The 13th Cusp;
Colors of India; Purple Haze;
A Silence of Echoes; Shorelines; Ekphrasticism;
Midnight Embers; Bridges and Clouds;
Inner Heart, a Journey; A Split in the Water

FREE e-books
Abstrusion; Wonderland; Fract & Flect;
Year of Divine Madness; 60 Haiku;
Midnight Shootout; Naked Leavings
The Rising; CJ Poetry & Paintings;

https://www.free-ebooks.net/search/candice+james

https://www.everand.com/author/572119332/Candice-James

10 PAK – 6

THE LONG POEMS

by
Candice James

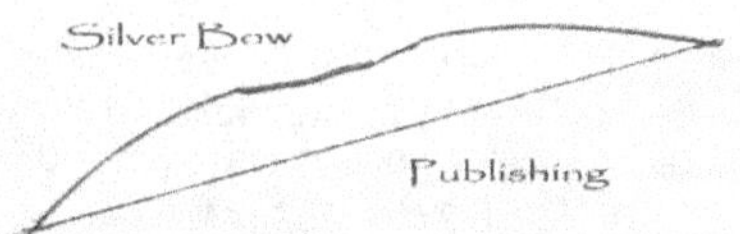

720 – 6th Street, Box # 5
New Westminster, BC
V3C 3C5   CANADA

Title: 10 PAK -6 The Long Poems
Author: Candice James
Copyright © 2026 Silver Bow Publishing
Cover Painting: "Snowy Dusk" painting by Candice James
Layout/Design: Candice James
ISBN: 978177403 397-5(print)
ISBN: 978177403 398-2 (ebk)

Library and Archives Canada Cataloguing in Publication
Title: 10 PAK-6: the long poems / by Candice James.
Other titles: Ten PAK-six Names: James, Candice, 1948- author. Identifiers: Canadiana (print) 20260108480 | Canadiana (ebook) 20260108499 | ISBN 9781774033975 (softcover) | ISBN 9781774033982 (Kindle) Subjects: LCGFT: Poetry. Classification: LCC PS8569.A429 A6126 2026 | DDC C811/.54—dc23

FOREWORD

The poems in this book are long poems set out in such a way as to allow the reader to rest on each page to fully digest the meaning and let their imagination run free to see the visuals and images the words are painting.

This layout gives the reader the best of experiences as they go through the poems and pages.

6

CONTENTS

8

The Hovering

10

Preface

A Soul crosses over in a haze into the arms of an angel helping it toward salvation. It is shown the consequences or rewards to be reaped by its potential actions in this strange magical transport that transpires in this mystical experience this side of life and the other side of death.

Dead in life. Alive in death.
Is not spoken of my breath.

It is an angel's presence
that hovers by my bed.
With tears of fear and dread
I fear I may be dead.

14

The angel's reassuring hand
is placed upon my brow.
A deadly fear possesses me
in this still here and now.

The angel's mouth did not move
but proceeded still to speak:
"Life's trials and tribulations
are for both the strong and meek."

I was rendered paralyzed
and could not move at all.
The angel eyes held me entranced.
I could not rise or fall.

A flash and I was lifted high
and sat upon a glittering stone.
I looked askance for kindred souls
but found I sat alone.

Golden chains clasped my wrists
and stripped me of all choice.
The angel opened up a book
and spoke in silken voice.

Embossed upon a gloss of film
I saw my lifetime pass,
and all my wins and all my sins
arose out of my past.

I was made to face myself
and weigh the right and wrong.
The sweet and sour of the notes
that played my earthly song.

17

The angel said we would survey
the measure of my soul.
Did it grow or did it shrink?
Was it diamond or black coal?.

Higher, higher, high we flew
above the clouds and stars.
I saw souls of golden hue
and dark ones behind bars.

As we traversed the endless skies
I came to understand;
all creatures great and small
are part of God's grand plan.

And thus, the angel spoke again.
I saw her small mouth move.
The edges hinted of a smile
her eyes could not disprove.

19

And as we tarried onward
a devil gave us chase.
Pursued by hooves of fury
we ran a deadly race.

If the angel was victorious
and the devil put asunder
my soul would be staid in grace
and safe inside God's wonder.

The silence cracked and then it split
and in one deadly breath
the devil was enflamed in fire
burnt in eternal death.

With feathered wings
and halo bright
the angel guided me
into the vibrant light.

We circled high above the scene
and the angel bid me look.
I saw a courtroom and a judge
and a sacred book.

I saw a mad demonic urchin
dressed and clad in blood and bone.
As scenes of his life were unwound
he began to writhe and moan.

He would be cast into hell
in fire and brimstone beyond score.
He would burn in hades wrath
eternally forevermore.

I watched and wondered of my fate.
Would I burn or would I freeze?
I felt myself begin to shake.
I buckled and fell to my knees.

And then there came a cooling mist
and on the hillside snow.
The burning fever left no scar.
I sank into the welcome cold.

A throng of angels gathered round
and I was both here and still there.
The moon and stars embraced the sun
and love and war deigned to play fair.

23

Then through the mist, the fading mist,
a figure of a saint shone through;
and I was blinded by the light
as blackest night turned to bright blue.

And I was here and I was there
as heaven's gate swung open wide.
With hope and glory everywhere
I was asked to step inside.

And oh, the glory of the moment.
The moment I had sought so long.
The grandeur and the shimmering
were birthing a new song.

I saw the orchestra tune up
to play an unknown symphony.
This new opera they played
foretold the death and birth of me.

And I was taken to a land
far beneath an emerald sea
where everything was fine and grand
and people lived in harmony.

The angel took me closer
so I could see who I could be,
now lodged in possibility,
that could turn to reality.

26

And then the scene dissolved
and I was in a darkened place.
I searched the fallen throng
to find a once familiar face.

But none in this place could be found.
This hellish cold and forlorn stone
was burning ice and melting frost.
The choice would be mine alone.

28

In heart or soul, on pearl or coal
I faced the path I'd led;
then in the morn I was reborn.
From a fresh womb I had been bled.

I was saved from fiery hell
and given one more chance
to sit redemption's recess out
or choose to have the dance.

30

I wakened from my lucid dream
as hazy ghosts dissolved.
My sins would be forgiven
and all my trials absolved.

It was an angel's presence
that hovered by my bed.

Joy and sorrow filled my head.
I was alive. I wasn't dead.

Dead in life. Alive in death,
is not spoken of my breath.

32

ACROSS DIMENSIONAL REALMS

Why are the stars nocturnal?
Privy to dawn and dusk
but always ... always
out of the sun's reach?

I call across dimensional realms
from inside a dystopian dream
adrift on an incarnate illusion
transcending life and breath
as I dance with death's
excommunicated twin brother
in a timeless
emptiness of emotion.

Within consciousness' unconscious
I am a paradox wrapped in a paradigm
existentially experiencing raw emotions,
sparring inside a juxtaposed reverie,
forever beginning and ending.

Hazing in and fading away
like the lost music of a familiar,
yet unfinished, symphony of strings.

I am constantly dreaming
yet always awake.
I am a second-hand perpetually moving
through the static clock of time
where hours, minutes and seconds
wander in place, but do not pass.

Where everything new is old
and everything antique is modern,
night parades surreptitiously beneath
a luminous sun that never eclipses,
cleansing the dark off all shadows,
silently demanding fealty to its radiance.

I am transforming into a starry night,
moving gracefully through a cosmic sky,
weaving magical, mystical reveries
into the ethereal universal essence.

I fluctuate and pulsate
in the twisted wrist of time.

I'm searching for an elusive kindness
that will absolve me of all my sins:
To grant me the gift of genuine compassion.
To show me how to forgive
those who have sinned against me.
That I may be forgiven my harmful actions
and reckless endangerment of others.

I am seeking reconciliation with myself.

How I long to enter other spirits' dreams
to see through their eyes and to feel
their emotions, desires and heartaches:

That I may come out of my shadows
into the light and be spiritually awakened
unto an inner-standing of my soul.

That I may not take
small miracles for granted.

That I may always be aware of them
and when they manifest,
in robust silence,
that I may hear them
above the noise of life.

Lord perfect me with limitless grace
and free me from worldly attachments.

Empower me in the baptism of truths.
Lift me up when my spirit falters.

Lay me on the unshakable foundation
of your endless encompassing love.

I have passed away from this realm
and am now alive in this inner death
held in the graces of heaven's embrace.

I am letting go of all my sorrows,
in the dawning of this dream state,
held in the smooth palm of timelessness.

A sublime silence permeates my essence.

I am uprooted from heaven's garden
and transported back to reality
where karma and kangaroos hold court
and a weary clown finds me guilty again.

42

I have served my sentence in iniquity
and am cleansed in the sacred waters
that flow above,
       below
  and all around me.

My parched spirit is restored once again.
I have left my barren awareness behind,
shed like a bear's cumbersome winter coat.

I'm now at one with myself and the world:
mindlessly following the blind,
calmly viewing this insane sanity,
trying to understand the madness.

The circle breaks and crumbles
and searches for its beginning:
becoming ... becoming ...
a thread in the gauze of infinity,
alive in the blue opaque mirror
of all my transparent spirit quests.

I am becoming ... becoming ...
a gentle echo of tranquil whispers.

I am becoming a ghost,
passing through violin strings,
vibrating an inner transcendence
where grace lays silently sleeping.

I have been a wandering wayfarer
unaware of past incarnations
and yet the past fragrances
of perfumed breezes I wandered through
have brought me to the undersea cemetery
of all my past memories:
pungent and alluring, innocuous and boring.

These out-carnations strive relentlessly
to become incarnate again.
They walk into and against the wind
seeking a familiar womb
in a void of limitless time
where all my existences live
and die and wait to be born again
into eventualities and incarnations
created in the womb of limitless love.

In this static state they still breathe
in their eternal thoughts and visions
unfolding and out-picturing themselves
into the matter of physical reality
and creating new universes
and multiverses, continuously,
and ever-evolving in timeless time.

Awake and dreaming in synchronicity,
we are the forever living paradoxes
grandiose and simple,
beautiful and plain.

Infinite, we ascend and transcend
in balanced, eloquent dance
proclaimed throughout the ages
in ageless poetry.

Eternalized and cherished
from the poetic written word
into the divine
then from the divine
 sprinkled back onto
the thirsty pages of pregnant prose.

In the depths of a fleeing dream
the essence of prayer
becomes transient
and becomes both life and death
dancing to nature's compelling rhythm
alive with mystic overtones
and magic spells
in the solemn aftermath of realization.

Inside the spark
residing in our flesh and bone body
timeless memories spin
on memory's reel of film.

Multidimensionality of spirit
is never ceasing; always evolving.
It is deeply encapsulated
in our synapses
emitting graceful electricity
that stretches
the elasticity of our consciousness
until we are past the point of now
and able to view the realm of then
from whence we have come
and where we are destined to return.

I hear a gentle humming in the air
and then a ringing in my ears
that demands to be heard.

I am aware, on some level,
that I am always being observed
on another level of consciousness
either by one of my other selves
or, perhaps, my very oversoul itself.

I am always being watched
by voyeurs in the oversoul committee.

I sometimes see a fleeting haze pass by.
But as quickly as I espy it,
it dissolves into the ether.

Sometimes I feel a heft in the mattress
as I am sleeping, half-awake,
but still aware of other-worldly things.

A spirit ghost from the realm beyond
has sat down on the bed where I lay
and I am left to wonder who it is.

I am certain it is a dead loved one
trying to let me know they are still near.

49

I swear I can hear
a gentle exhalation of breath
and I feel a tingling in my soul
so deep and strong
that it manifests
goosepimples on my flesh
and a chill runs through my spirit.

And, just as reality begins to fade
into blessed oblivion,
I feel a shiver rising up
from deep within me.

A jolt of some kind of *'otherness'* steps in
and reminds me I am still here
and the dead, although near,
are still not here.

I am alone in my loneliness once again.
I feel a hush crawling over the whispers
I am trying to birth into a sound
then a word, then a sentence.

But nothing comes.

Silence expands, clings, smothers.

And the age-old unanswerable question
from yesterday resurfaces
again, and again and again:

Why are the stars nocturnal?
Privy to dawn and dusk
but always ... always
out of the sun's reach?

A SPARK

52

53

Divorced from understanding
     and empathy
I'm a lost soul in an orphaned sea
but a spark of your soul
still lives in me.

54

I would try to coax your affections
with the sleight of sympathy's balm
but you, in your all-knowing
disheveled ambivalence
and ever-wavering wanton wisdom,
would feel
the disharmony and discord
in my soul
and the lack of sentiment.

How I long to see this dystopian reality
become transcended via your love
into a quiet and fashionable utopia

How I long to deliver a gentleness,
to the heartbroken and forgotten.

How I long to live in your eyes
　　past the tenth of forever.

    I am restless
in the presence of my absence
trying to come to terms with my ghost
in a strange, majestic hall of ordinances
deprived of coveted gentleness and sighs.

    Dead to the living and yet,
alive with an innocence craving devotion,
I lay down to sleep on a carpet
of fresh, winter frost and white ice
that warms my soul to a cinder.

Here beneath a sultry copper sky
I turn to gold in your embrace.

So beautiful,
your image shines throughout.

Inside these dulled eyes you still gleam
like a shimmering dewdrop on a rose.

I peer through its luminescence
and enter in ethereal mist
into the deepest eye of your need.
and bathe in the silky brilliance
of your surreal abstract love.

And then the cold reality
of your continued absence
creeps into the bright
and paints it black.

The night grows long
and never ends
    and then
the longest longing begins.

Here I long for you to come to me
and assuage my fears and tears.
I pray I've not fallen from your grace
and not been expunged from your heart.

I pray the layer of my love's paint
has not been exposed to
the turpentine barbs of loneliness'
that knock on the door of your soul
while we endure this disinterment
from each other's quantum soul.

I walk alone along this desolate beach
and I would, that I could,
be the sands that sift thought your hands
and caress you yearning soul
to the point of expiation
that we may melt inside each other
once again in this annihilation
of nihilism and sectarianism.

I will put on my poker face
and let the chips fall where they may
knowing all roads lead to you
and the dice are loaded
and headed to the celestial star
    where you are.

And I am burning
with favor and fever
to die in your arms once again
to be reborn unto myself
          as I am.

The viciousness of your innocence
whets my desire with intrinsic fire
and I am justified in my pursuit
of a righteousness that burns
and yearns for exoneration of guilt
erroneously attributed to my fall
from the perilous crimes of the heart
into the grace of your charms.
to receive validation that I am
and always will be the only one
you live and breathe for.

64

That throughout eternity
through incarnations and karma
I am your mother, your father,
your brother, your sister,
your son and your daughter
and every grandchild
you've ever known.

Yes, throughout eternity,
I have always been your all
and your everything;
but most of all
I am forever the only one
you've ever lived and breathed for.

In this series of eternalism
we have never been estranged.

In the age of woke apparitioning
you will never be a ghost to me.
I've loved you all my lives;
even long before we ever met.

A spark of your soul is,
and has always been,
burning inside
the deep of my soul.

HERE

71

Here, in the optical illusion
of a twilight long since dead,
I pay homage to the living spark
of my indestructible soul
        as I resurrect
    the dream we are.

A million years collide with
the minutes and seconds
of all my days and nights
spent inside timeless time.

Time that passes itself
as it does not pass.

I am "the I am."
A never-ending circle
without beginning or end.

Each and every degree
is all the other degrees.
Exactly the same in their plurality
and at the same time
single in their singularity.

Here, inside this spectrum
of imagined pearled moons,
I count the scattering stars.

Silver eggs that will not crack;
they brighten the dark of night
in evanescent mirrored sequins
askew on a black velvet canvas.

As they wink at the cosmic winds
the guardian of the skies
anoints their flirtatious eyes
with a wet luminescent teardrop
to tempt the distant galaxies
into eternity's universal dance.

76

I spin a web of tantalizing wonder
where shimmers slink and slide down
the spinal cord of midnight's back.

I see the ghosts of my past
coming alive in a swirling mist.
I whisper to the winds of change
awaiting my new sojourn.

I wait here in this elusive dream state
recalling past joys and sorrows,
past successes and dismal failures,
smiling and frowning,
weeping and laughing
as they become the mellowed sails
that cling to my ship's mast;
that I may reconcile
my joys and sorrows
into a feasible mathematical equation
that will not disprove my worth.

Here, in my most secret reveries,
I believe my past is catching up
          to my present
and will eventually become my future
as all time passes within itself

     — not passing at all —
       just simply being.

No more will it separate us, alienate us,
censure us and dis-indenture us
and leave us totally disentangled
in the quantum field that enfolds us.

The one we called our own
before the night tides became
uncontrolled tsunamis of destruction
and ripped me from myself
and from my universe
into an inky entangled world
of misconception and deception.

Out of the night that covers me
in my cocoon of forgetfulness
a blinding light invades my dark.

Is it a star exploding?
Or a cosmic cryogenic implosion
on a distant expiring universe
encroaching on the eastern edge
of the western rim
of my sentient eclipse?

82

Is it just starlit clip of yesterday?
Or a blip, on time that is not time,
lost in a blurred cinematic scope?

83

Incarcerated
in a jail of tidal waters
I drown
in vain then drown again.

A golden pendulum
of ultimate truths
sways back and forth
on heaven's swing,
whispering
of sin's repercussions.

85

Here, in the optical illusion
of a twilight long since dead,
I pay homage to the living spark
of our indestructible souls
and resurrect the dream we are
again, and again and again.

I Am #1725

A harsh wind saunters in
on sky-blue high heel slippers
calling my name in soft whispers.

A thin rain falls
from the fluttering eyelids
of war weary storm clouds
as they scatter into the scarce
and the scratch of my reverie.

I haze into the vortex of my soul.
I materialize and manifest
as a surreal, blurred ghost
wandering the shoreline and shallows
of my childhood memories
and yesterday whispers.

There is definitely a musicality
to the images and atmosphere.

And my mother,
my dear, dear mother and I
are always there, together,
wading the edge of the ocean
glistening beneath a hot July sun.

A seagull keens overhead,
soars and dips through the waves,
in a surreal dissolving weave.

And in the surreal
weave of the waves
I hear my mother singing
"I'll Be Seeing You."

I close my eyes
and feel her near me
and I see her smiling at me
   through the thin
     of the veil.

Then the sky cracks open
and a thick rain falls
pounding the sand into pock marks:
— a gray pimpled face dissolving —
    in the wake of my tears.

I watch my mother slowly fading,
    ebbing into the waves,
fragmenting then dissolving
    disappearing then gone
    almost like she never was.

And I'm still here
almost like I never am.

I am #1725 of 1728 here ...
when I am here.

When I am there,
in the other-verse,
I speak in languages
unknown to me here.

But somewhere
    in between
the vast ever changing
    in between
I know all my selves
and I am fluent
in all their languages
            and
a part of them all.

A small unseasonal whippoorwill
sings a song for only me
and somewhere in between
we share a wistful sigh
for all that was and wasn't
and all the could-have-beens
that never came to pass.

But still, I remain unfazed.
I remain, branded and stamped
with a new soul and spirit
in an unspecified dream
with no "best before" date.
I am # 1725 of 1728
with 3 more sojourns to complete,

I am the remaining.
I am the unfazed.

I am # 1725

GHOST

In the blue of a golden moment
a fluorescent thought appears
and holds court.

The pings and pongs of the tennis ball,
as it whispers to the net in passing,
transfuse the air with expectation
chilling creation's inspiration.

It's just that kind of day,
When the gold turns to pearl;
then to emerald to silver.

The sword of the sun
cuts through the quick of day.
The curtain of night falls;
and the moon plays solitaire
with a scatter of stars
as they ride their trail of dust
into a sky-high sea of black.

A guided hush weaves its way
through a lonely crowd of one
fine tuning the dial of dreams
to FM for forgotten memories
and AM for audio moments.

Yesterday paintings cascade,
in film noire clips,
framing a nostalgic parade
of blurred passageways
that lead to nowhere again.

The hush begins to fade,
in reality's cool breath,
and the images blur and smear
in the foggy mist
becoming snow-kissed
in time's luxurious embrace.

Sunshine inside the rain.
Tears inside the sundrops.

The road is long and winding
and then it drops into the sea
or dissolves into the sky.

And I sit in patient silence
miming the name of the Lord
          enmeshed
in a forest of forgiveness.

Through a cloud of powdered mist
          I see you
nonchalantly approaching.

You don't seem to see me.

I move toward you.
As I embrace you,
you pass through me.

For a moment I am puzzled;
then I realize
you are a ghost.

But, then,
I realize
you are not.

I am the ghost
lost to your reality.

Slowly you dissolve
then disappear
as the door between us
   Closes.

Amassing ...
inside a cruel congregation
tears and fears ebb and flow.

Pleated curtains
turn into knives
and the floor becomes
a quicksand mire.

Dangling electrified wires
chase me down an endless hall
where portraits come alive
and mime the names of the dead.

I feel a cold sweat
creeping through me.

Moisture droplets
bead on my bible.

My prayer book
becomes blurred ink.

116

I know I have a favorite prayer
but I can't recall how it begins
or what testament it is in.

Moving through
my beleaguered body
are towels for my tears
and salve for my soul
as I begin to wend my way home.

118

I am moving through doors,
swinging past stars
and passing through ghosts
that are not ghosts,
because —

I am the ghost ...

I am the ghost.

A Fool's Paradise

I have travelled
over hills and dales,
forests and deserts,
rivers, lakes and oceans
and
the formidable mountains
of timeless time

I have travelled
smiles and tears
for years and years
on a lonely highway
of darkness and stars
in search of another time,
another place,
another reality.

Coming back
into this reality,
I'm climbing
through the keyhole
of a fading blurred yesterday
to pass through
the eye of today
as I search for the key
to an elusive tomorrow
that may never come to pass.

I am a theatre
under the stars
playing in
a vaguely familiar movie.

Lights, camera, action
and there I am.

The am I am, are, is, was.

127

My images
pass through each other
as ghosts
on a near miss collision course
of familiar faces
in a series of
divine comedy-dramas

I am living and I am dead
in the abstraction
of surreal eternity
shaking the rose petals
from a blushing bush.

The leaves shudder
in echoes of tears
flooding the soil
with silent screams.

I walk the passages of time:
past, present, future
and pluperfect.

Unafraid, yet aware,
I am not at peace.

A stale vibrance
permeates the air.

A cloyed clutch
burgeons and births
into a pulsating pocket
of exquisite air.

It is the autumn
of summer's fall.
It is the spring
of winter's inheritance.

It is interchangeable
impossibility
and a possibility
ever-changing.

Cradled in the womb of time
I hear drums and music
rewriting the score
for the dances I am
and the new dances
I will need to learn.

And all the while,
life dances in the chorus line
of a beleaguered
long ago burnt-out cabaret
where I am searching
for embers and sparks
to light up the dark
while I sing torch songs
to a past I can't reclaim.

I am reborn
and reborn and reborn
again, and again and again:
Learning new moves
and deep dances.
Living in the rapture
of a song I love.

But, alas, I've lost the words
so, I'm humming and miming
song after song after song
hoping to find that part of me
I lost in the search for redemption.

Coming back into this reality,
I am lost in an oblivion
of want and need and desire
not realizing that sometimes
redemption is only a pipe dream
for paupers and poltroons
            and...
    it never comes.

But still,
I wait for it,
beneath a paper moon,
here
in a fool's paradise.

139

Raindrops

140

I close my eyes
and listen to my breath
trying to identify
that momentary stillness
   cleft in between
     the in-between.

Adrift in a sea of dominoes
on a checkerboard ocean
of half played lives
      I stand
in soft warm rain.

142

And there,
at the edge of my vision,
I'm suddenly aware of
approaching ghosts.

Some know my name.
Some are strangers.

I walk, gingerly,
with uncertainty's wisdom
between battered pillars
and burning posts.

Feeling the flame.
Aware of the dangers.

Inside a thinned crowd of people
I am an insignificant figure
hazing in and out,

I peer
t h r o u g h
a rain rippled window.

Everything moving stands still;
and everything static
seems to move.

Raindrops are
clear, transparent liquid.
Solid wet things
dripping from the sky.

But when they fall
they disappear at the touch
like a windblown kiss
that never arrives.

Half-alive and dreaming,
half-asleep and dead,
I am a ghostly wayfarer
hanging by a thread.

The raindrops
have been tucked inside
the pockets of the sun.

Inside the whisper of a hush
I slowly come undone.

Redemption's Caress

151

Goodbye blue house of heaven.
Hello red door of life.
Farewell the dreamer's dreamings.
Hello, the dream I am.

My thoughts unveil.
My costume dissolves
in the tears and smiles
of timeless time.

153

Goodbye old memories,
cravings and heart throbs.
Hello new creation,
inspiration and dreams.

154

I drink from the wine
of sacred seduction
and sleep in the palm
of redemption's caress.

Finally,
at long last,

I'm at one
with
the eternal now.

FISTFULS
OF
MOONGLOW

158

Carrying fistfuls of moonglow,
I walk through
the star dusted streets
with the dead
that come to my door.

They swim effortlessly
through the dark waters of time
    seeking the cool
of my winter blue eyes
as they cast off the heat
of summer's *stale* embrace.

They are the masters
    of black fire
and indelible, indigo flame.

162

They shine in shards of mirror,
reflecting kaleidoscope years,
pouring memories
and dark water
into the heel of my heart.

Carrying fistfuls of moonglow,
I lay at the altar of the lost
near the crossroads of death.

The moonglow
shimmers and pulsates
in the soft clench
of my fists.

I leave the star dusted streets
with only the imprint of my footsteps
in the fading drops of moonglow
as the dead
dissolve in the mist ...

whispering,
almost inaudibly —
auf wiedersehen.

AUTHOR PROFILE

Candice James is a professional poet, musician, singer, songwriter and visual artist. She was appointed Poet Laureate Emerita of New Westminster BC by order if City Council in November 2016 after serving 2 back-to-back three-year terms as Poet Laureate. She is founder of Royal City Literary Arts Society, and Fred Cogswell Award For Excellence in Poetry; and past president of the Federation of BC Writers. She's a full member of the League of Canadian Poets and the author of 34 books of poetry through 6 Publishing Houses.

Her first book A SPLIT IN THE WATER was published in 1979 by Fiddlehead Poetry Books, University of New Brunswick CANADA. (2nd edition Silver Bow Publishing 2025) Her awards include Pandora's Collective Citizen of the Year; Bernie Legge Platinum Awards Artist of the Year. She is a 'Life Member" of Royal City Literary Arts Society.

https://www.silverbowpublishing.com/candice-james.html